ONE COW MOO MOO!

Written by David Bennett
Illustrated by Andy Cooke

Henry Holt and Company
New York

For William
D.B.
For Rosi
A.C.

Text copyright © 1990 by David Bennett.
Illustrations copyright © 1990 by Andy Cooke.
All rights reserved, including the right to reproduce
this book or portions thereof in any form.

Created and produced by
David Bennett Books Ltd,
94 Victoria Street, St Albans,
Herts, AL1 3TG,
England

Published by Henry Holt and Company, Inc.,
115 West 18th Street, New York, New York 10011.
Published in Canada by Fitzhenry & Whiteside Limited,
195 Allstate Parkway, Markham, Ontario L3R 4T8.

Library of Congress Cataloging-in-Publication Data
Bennett, David.
One cow, moo, moo / by David Bennett ; illustrated by Andy Cooke.
Summary: Introduces the numbers one through ten as a puzzled
little boy watches a succession of animals rush by.
ISBN 0-8050-1416-0
[1. Counting. 2. Animals—Fiction. 3. Stories in rhyme.]
I. Cooke, Andy, ill. II. Title
PZ8.3.B4380n 1990
[E]-dc20.   90-32065

Henry Holt books are available at special discounts
for bulk purchases for sales promotions, premiums,
fund-raising, or educational use. Special editions
or book excerpts can also be created to specification.

For details contact:
Special Sales Director
Henry Holt & Company, Inc.
115 West 18th Street
New York, New York 10011

First Edition

Printed in Hong Kong

1   3   5   7   9   10   8   6   4   2

ONE COW MOO MOO!

I saw one cow go running by.
It said,
"MOO MOO!"
I wonder why.

I saw two horses go running by.
They said,
"NEIGH NEIGH!"
I wonder why.
They chased the cow
that said, "MOO MOO!"

I saw three donkeys go running by.
They said,
"HEE HAW!"
I wonder why.
They chased the horses
that chased the cow
that said, "MOO MOO!"

I saw four pigs go running by.
They said,
"OINK OINK!"
I wonder why.
They chased the donkeys
that chased the horses
that chased the cow
that said, "MOO MOO!"

I saw five hens go running by.
They said,
"CLUCK CLUCK!"
I wonder why.
They chased the pigs
that chased the donkeys
that chased the horses
that chased the cow
that said, "MOO MOO!"

5

I saw six geese go running by.
They said,
"HONK HONK!"
I wonder why.
They chased the hens
that chased the pigs
that chased the donkeys
that chased the horses
that chased the cow
that said, "MOO MOO!"

I saw seven sheep go running by.
They said,
"BAA BAA!"
I wonder why.
They chased the geese
that chased the hens
that chased the pigs
that chased the donkeys
that chased the horses
that chased the cow
that said, "MOO MOO!"

I saw eight dogs go running by.
They said,
"WOOF WOOF!"
I wonder why.
They chased the sheep
that chased the geese
that chased the hens
that chased the pigs
that chased the donkeys
that chased the horses
that chased the cow
that said, "MOO MOO!"

I saw nine cats go running by.
They said,
"MEOW MEOW!"
I wonder why.
They chased the dogs
that chased the sheep
that chased the geese
that chased the hens
that chased the pigs
that chased the donkeys
that chased the horses
that chased the cow
that said, "MOO MOO!"

I saw ten mice go running by.
They said,
"SQUEAK SQUEAK!"
I wonder why.
They chased the cats
that chased the dogs
that chased the sheep
that chased the geese
that chased the hens
that chased the pigs
that chased the donkeys
that chased the horses
that chased the cow
that said, "MOO MOO!"

Then I saw why
ten mice went by,
that chased nine cats
that chased eight dogs
that chased seven sheep
that chased six geese
that chased five hens
that chased four pigs
that chased three donkeys
that chased two horses
that chased one cow
that said, "MOO MOO!"